# PARADE!

## BY TOM SHACHTMAN ★ PHOTOGRAPHS BY CHUCK SAAF

### MACMILLAN PUBLISHING COMPANY ★ NEW YORK

The author and photographer wish to give special thanks to Macy's Special Productions team for their extensive cooperation during all phases of work on this book, and to the *Williamsport Area High School in Williamsport, Pennsylvania*, for its warm hospitality.

Macmillan Publishing Company
866 Third Avenue, New York, NY 10022
Collier Macmillan Canada, Inc.

Printed in the United States of America

10  9  8  7  6  5  4  3  2  1

Library of Congress Cataloging in Publication Data
Shachtman, Tom, date.
Parade!

Summary: Text and photographs present the annual Macy's Thanksgiving Day Parade in New York City.
1. Parades—New York (N.Y.)—Juvenile literature.
2. Thanksgiving Day—Juvenile literature. (1. Parades.
2. Thanksgiving Day) I. Saaf, Chuck, ill. II. Title.
GT4011.N7S53    1985    394.5'09747'1    85–7308
ISBN 0-02-782540-X

PICTURE CREDITS: All photographs are by Chuck Saaf except for the following: pages 4 and 5, Courtesy of The New York Public Library, The Branch Libraries, Picture Collection; pages 6 and 7, copyright © 1925, 1926, 1929, 1930, 1931, 1935 R. H. Macy & Co., Inc., Courtesy of Macy's Thanksgiving Day Parade; page 24 (top), "Underdog" balloon © Leonardo-TTV, photograph copyright © 1985 Chuck Saaf; page 25, "Raggedy Ann" balloon © 1984 Character Licensing, Inc., photograph copyright © 1984 R. H. Macy & Co., Inc., Courtesy of Macy's Thanksgiving Day Parade; page 38 (top, left and right) and page 39, photographs by Mariette Pathy Allen, copyright © 1984 R. H. Macy & Co., Inc., Courtesy of Macy's Thanksgiving Day Parade; pages 12 (bottom), 15 (right), 16, 17 (both), 27 (both), 28 (all), 29 (both), 30, 31, 34 (all), 36 (bottom right), 40, 50 (left, top and bottom), 59 (bottom right) copyright © 1985 Tom Shachtman.

Macmillan books are available at special discounts for bulk purchases for sales promotions, premiums, fund raising, or educational use. For details, contact:

Special Sales Director
Macmillan Publishing Company
866 Third Avenue

In New York City the November day is bright and cold, filled with expectation and excitement. It's early on Thanksgiving morning.

Soon, at precisely nine o'clock, the 58th Annual Macy's Thanksgiving Day Parade will begin.

Two million spectators will line the route. At home, over eighty million Americans will watch the parade on television.

In this year's parade, nearly five thousand people will take part. There will be nine enormous balloons, eighteen large floats and many smaller ones, a dozen of the country's best marching bands, clowns by the hundreds, float and balloon attendants, stars from Hollywood and the sports world, and cartoon characters.

The parade is about to begin. Each year there are different balloons, floats, and bands. But all are part of a parade tradition that goes back thousands of years.

People have probably been making parades since time immemorial. Pictures of stately processions and military units marching in rows can be seen on the walls of ancient pyramids in Egypt, Mexico, and Asia. Two thousand years ago, in the Roman Empire, parades celebrated army victories and pagan holidays.

*Bottom left: Decorated elephants. India, 1650*
*Bottom right: St. George and the Dragon. England, 1615*

Modern parade tradition really began about five hundred years ago, during the Middle Ages and the Renaissance. Most processions were religious in nature, but some celebrated special seasons of the year or great occasions like the entry of a king into a city. The word *parade* was invented then, in France; it meant a "preparing" for a celebration, or a "showing off" of finery, acrobatics, and marching ability. General merrymaking came to be a part, as well.

In the United States, a St. Patrick's Day parade has been held since before the Revolutionary War, and the New Orleans Mardi Gras and Philadelphia Mummers' festivals date from the turn of the twentieth century. All include elaborate costumes, handmade carriages or floats, and puppets that are larger than life.

*Top left: Wedding procession.*
*Florence, Italy, 1579*
*Bottom left: German ambassador*
*visits Moscow, Russia, 1698*

Top left: 1925; bottom right: 1926

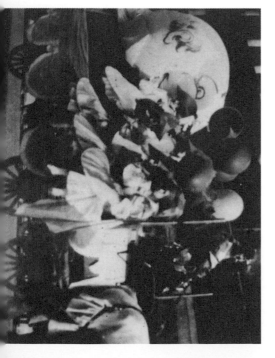

The first Macy's Thanksgiving Day Parade was held in 1924, and about a thousand of the New York department store's employees marched in it. Many of them had recently come to this country from Europe, and they missed the holiday festivals of the countries where they were born. The parade served to remind them of their roots, celebrated an American holiday, and also announced the approach of the Christmas season.

Its success encouraged Macy's, and, except for a few years during World War II, the parade has been an annual event ever since. Early parades started from 110th Street and went nearly five miles down Broadway to Herald Square—an exhausting march. The route was later shortened to a bit over two miles. In 1927 Macy's asked theatrical designer Tony Sarg to create the first of the huge rubber balloons that have become the procession's hallmark.

Year by year the parade grew in size and scope. Star performers from the Broadway theater and from Hollywood were added. The parade was carried live on radio in the 1930s and has been an annual television special since the late 1940s. Traditions grew as Macy's employees passed on their roles in the parade within departments or store groups. Former employees often asked to be allowed to march, long after they had left the Macy's family. Today the Macy's Thanksgiving Day Parade is a spectacular event, one of the greatest of all holiday celebrations in the United States.

*Top left: 1929; middle: 1930; bottom: 1931. Top right: 1935*

Though the parade takes place on a single day, it is the result of a year-long effort by a great many people. Macy's Special Productions department, a team of professional experts, is responsible for the creative planning of the parade, and for working with the volunteer Parade Committee of employees on the million-and-one details of the event.

Parade Director Jean McFaddin says, "The parade is Macy's gift to the families of the country; it brings out the child in everyone."

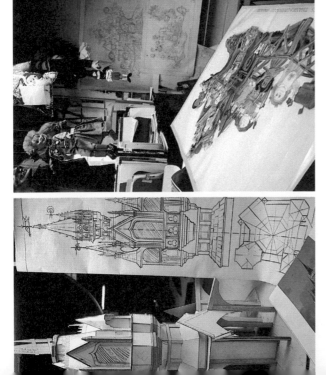

Nine new parade floats start to come to life as early as the January before the parade, at Macy's construction studio in Hoboken, New Jersey. Here ideas are translated into sketches, blueprints, models, and —finally—rolling fantasy wagons.

Each float is a theater-in-the-round. It serves as a mobile stage platform for performances and will be watched from many angles.

Carpenters, sculptors, welders, painters, and other craftsmen and craftswomen work together on the new floats. Some of the floats are sponsored by various American companies. The floats feature various children's characters, such as the "Cabbage Patch Kids," or themes of general interest, such as the Statue of Liberty.

Manfred Bass, chief float designer and head of the studio, says the Thanksgiving Day parade "brings out the imaginative part of the soul." He hopes his designs will "make people forget about the everyday world and enjoy the holiday." Manfred and Bobby Davidowski have been building for the parade for twenty years.

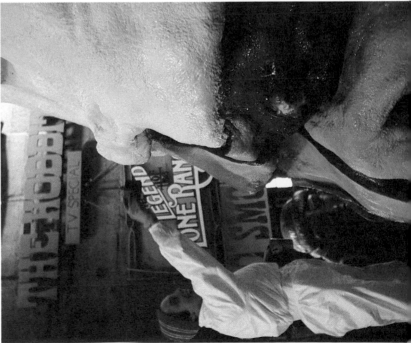

The making of parade floats comes from an American tradition of carving and metal-working that was in full flower about one hundred years ago. Forebears of the artisans in the Macy's studio carved cigar-store figures and ship models, painted signs, and cast metal carousel horses and circus wagons. Today the workers' materials include plexiglass, foam, fabric, and light metals, as well as wood and iron.

It is not enough simply to make the floats eye-catching and sturdy. Each must also be designed so that it can be folded into a small size for the trip on Thanksgiving morning through the Lincoln Tunnel from New Jersey into New York City.

The construction requires painstaking attention to detail. The floats will take several months to complete, and each will be the product of many hands.

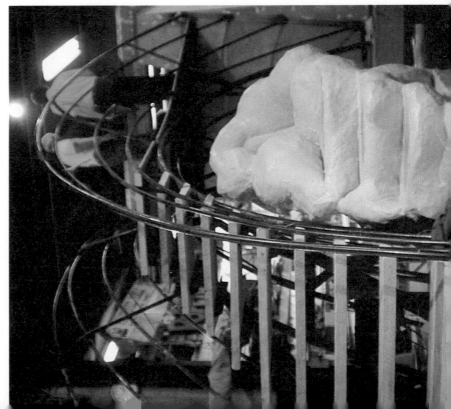

While the floats are being built in the studio, the Special Productions unit at Macy's Herald Square store in New York City is a beehive of activity. Bands and celebrity performers must be chosen. Balloons must be decided upon. Costumes must be made.

About 2,500 employees from seventeen stores, and their families, will take part in the parade. Applications pour in from all those who want to march. Sometimes it seems that everyone wants to be a clown!

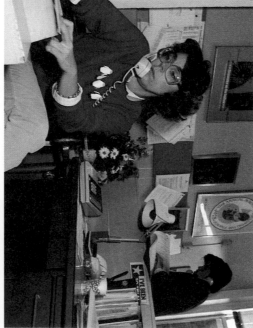

The Parade Committee must arrange for such things as transportation, housing, and food for those who will work on or in the parade. These matters might seem to have little to do with marching, but they are essential to the success of the event.

Many volunteers work behind the scenes and on the sidelines to make this once-a-year event go smoothly. Each group of marchers, each balloon and float and band, will be accompanied by a parade official—a captain or a marshal—wearing a distinctive blazer.

Employees who have held leadership positions on the parade for six years receive an award called a *Rollie*, after Rowland H. Macy, founder of the department store.

One of the hardest tasks at Special Productions is to pick the twelve bands that will march and perform in the parade. There are over three hundred applicants each year. Each band that applies sends in video and audio cassettes of its performances to be reviewed.

Only one band will be chosen from any one state. A wide geographical spread is the goal. And once a band has appeared in the parade, it must wait several years before reapplying to march.

The twelve invited bands are mostly from high schools and are among the very best in the nation. Many have won major band competitions and have performed in the Rose Bowl or Cotton Bowl festivals. In past years, bands have come from as far away as Hawaii and England. This year there are bands from Texas, New Mexico, Florida, and Indiana—to name just a few states.

One band that has never come to the Macy's parade before is the "Marching Millionaires" of Williamsport, Pennsylvania. On an afternoon in September, band director Paul Kellerman stands atop the Williamsport Area High School to coach a practice session of the band and drill team. The Millionaires have won three Atlantic Coast regional championships in the last four years.

In Williamsport, and in many other schools that field championship bands, band members spend as much time practicing as do varsity football players. Rehearsals begin during the summer, and practice sessions are held four days a week after school. Band members also attend instrumental classes each day, and on weekends they travel to football games and competitions.

The Williamsport girls' drill team works closely with director Janet Herrick. Twenty girls hold and flip wooden rifles, and forty more twirl several different sets of flags during the band's twelve-minute shows at football games.

Cooperation, paying attention to instructions, and a willingness to put in long hours all help to shape a championship band. Because the hard work pays off in excellence, band members agree that the effort is worthwhile.

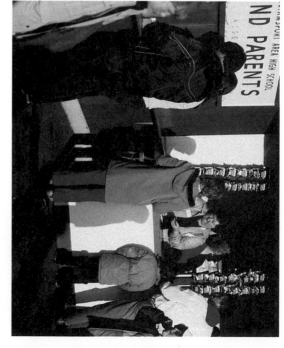

The Band Parents Association regularly supports the marchers by running refreshment stands at football games and doing many other chores.

At the turn of the century, Williamsport had more millionaires than any other city in Pennsylvania—hence, the name of the band, Marching Millionaires. But today the city is not so wealthy, and raising money to send the band to New York for a two-day Thanksgiving and parade experience became a major project.

During the summer, the popular group "The Beach Boys" performed in Williamsport and donated money for the band's trip. Civic groups pitched in. There was an auction. And, on this weekend in September, the band is giving a public concert and the downtown merchants are contributing a percentage of their sales to the fund.

When the Millionaires strut onto the football field for a twilight performance, they can feel that the whole town is behind their efforts.

While the bands are practicing and the floats are being built, the six-story-high balloons begin to come to life.

In the history of the parade, there have been ninety-seven different balloons. New ones are added, and old ones are retired, each year. Recently Macy's has taken over the design and maintenance of the giant characters, and is working with various contractors to construct them.

First, a pattern must be made. Then each small section, such as a foot or a hand, is cut out of urethane-coated nylon. Each section is individually sealed before the sections are sealed together into a whole balloon. Test inflations are made at every step.

The balloon is built in sections so that if during the parade it hits an obstacle such as a light pole, only a small section may deflate, and the balloon will still be able to continue to the end. After the balloon is completed, it is hand painted.

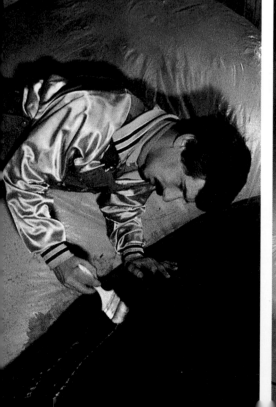
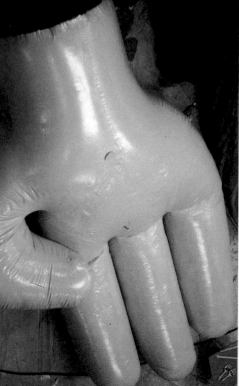
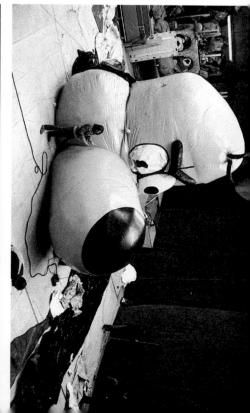

Test flights for new balloons are a must. "Raggedy Ann" has to get up and fly right! Afterward, the balloon is deflated and stored by Macy's in Hoboken, until the night before the parade.

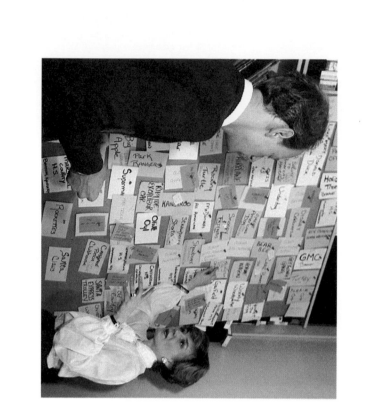

As the date for the parade nears, the Special Productions team works on the order for the procession. Each band, float, balloon, and group of clowns is represented on the bulletin board by a small card. Should a band with green uniforms march next to the green "Kermit the Frog" balloon? Should the "Care Bears" float be far away from the "Yogi Bear" balloon?

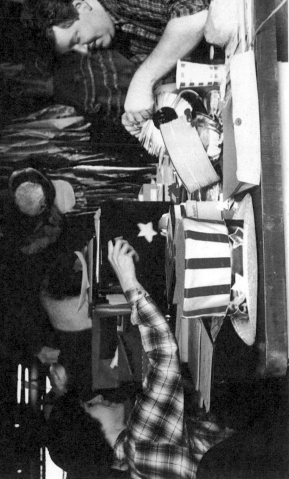

Many other details remain to be settled. The clowns must be taught how to perform. Balloon handlers must practice working together as teams. There are a thousand questions to be answered. When should a limousine go to the airport to pick up the stars of NBC's "Hill Street Blues" who are appearing in the parade? Have all the light poles along the line of march been turned around so they won't snag a balloon? Have the roads been checked and potholes fixed so no unexpected jolts will upset a finely balanced float? Do the bus drivers bringing employees to the parade from the Macy's store in Albany know where to park at six in the morning?

Parade planning has to be coordinated with NBC, which broadcasts the parade, with the New York City Police Department and several other city agencies, and with hundreds of other organizations and interested parties.

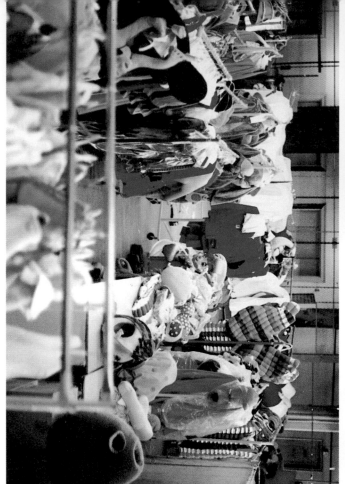

On this Saturday, twelve days before the parade, those who are going to march in it come to the eighteenth floor of the Herald Square store to try on their costumes and to learn how to move in them.

Each costume is individually fitted to its wearer. Time is taken now to make final adjustments. When everyone returns here to dress on the morning of the parade, there will not be a moment to spare.

In one corner of the floor, choreographers work with the marchers. These professional dancers and dance designers teach each small group how to do the few steps that they will perform, over and over again, along the parade route. The dance pattern for each group of float attendants is different. Practice makes perfect!

Masks, anyone? Who would you like to be?

Only a few more days to go!
A group of Head Start children from near-
by Union City, New Jersey, and some press
people come to the Hoboken construction
studio for a viewing of the completed floats.

On Wednesday, the last day before the parade, bands are traveling toward the parade from all over the country. Most of the youngsters, including those from Williamsport, Pennsylvania, have never been to New York City before. Are all the flags packed?

It's the night before the parade. In a few hours, the procession will begin. Preparations are already under way on 77th Street, as well as at Herald Square.

At seven in the evening, rehearsals start for the NBC cameras in front of the Macy's building at Herald Square. The red star marks the spot!

The parade is not only a march, it is also a live television show that takes an enormous amount of planning. As Macy's gets the parade program into final shape, NBC becomes involved in staging the entertainment, visiting the bands to determine camera angles, surveying the floats and dance numbers. Dick Schneider has produced and directed the NBC broadcast of the parade for many years.

NBC cameras will cover the starting line of the parade, but most of them will be concentrated at Herald Square, where the marching units will give performances aimed especially at the television audience.

Rehearsals at Herald Square will go on through the night.

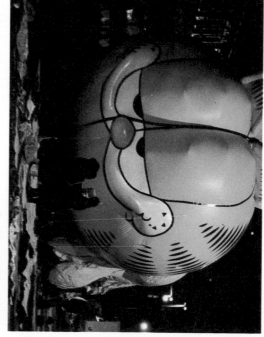

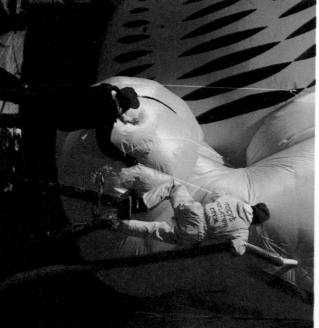

Meanwhile, on 77th Street, outside the American Museum of Natural History, the balloons are being inflated. Weather reports are checked to see what sort of day tomorrow will be, and the helium-and-air mixture for the balloons is adjusted accordingly. Once inflated, each balloon is held down by ropes, canvas, and sandbags.

Through the night, the inflation work continues and the excitement builds.

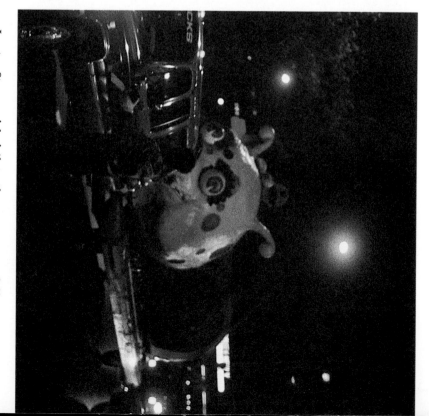

Just after midnight, the convoy of floats begins to arrive.

The floats come to rest in parade order along Central Park West and 81st Street. Those that are more difficult to assemble are opened up first. Cranes and a volunteer crew assist the studio experts in putting them together. Teamwork is essential.

When most of the city is fast asleep, there is a feeling of hushed anticipation around the museum. Only a few more hours before dawn!

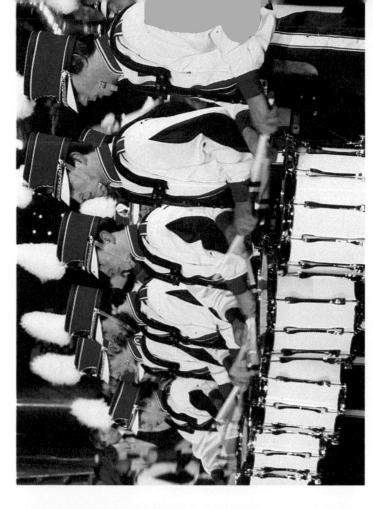

But at Herald Square at 4:30 A.M., the noise level is as high as the sky. All twelve bands are rehearsing, one after another. Is anybody sleepy?

At 5:30 A.M., hundreds of men, women, and children start arriving on the eighteenth floor of the Macy's Herald Square store to get ready for the parade. Make-up is applied by student make-up artists. Everyday faces and clothes disappear; in their places are bursts of color and movement.

A gaggle of clowns goes down the freight elevator and boards a bus for the museum. In the next three hours, dozens of buses will shuttle back and forth between the store and the parade's starting line.

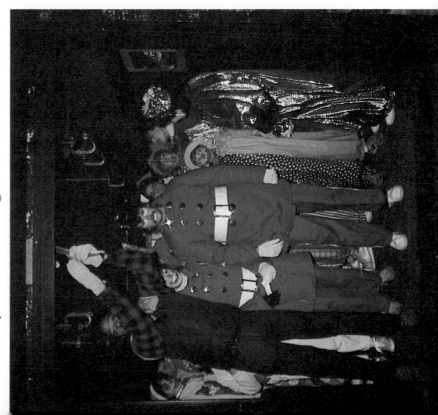

As darkness yields to dawn, the hubbub on 77th Street and around the museum rises faster than the sun. Thanksgiving Day is going to be cold and glorious, a perfect day for a parade.

Moment by moment, more and more people pour into the starting area. Busloads of bands. Throngs of balloon handlers. Float escorts practicing their dance steps. Hundreds of clowns. Some Macy's employees have come from as far away as Florida. Many people from nearer points have brought children.

Along the route, the crowds begin to settle themselves as well. They know the show will be worth the wait.

Eight o'clock. This is the hour for last-minute meetings, for consultations with the heads of police department squadrons, for testing out communications links. Marshals and captains join their groups. They will keep the units marching in the right order, and will maintain proper spacing.

Everyone hurries to his or her place, and muscles are stretched for the march. The last few minutes of waiting are almost unbearable.

The whole long year of working and waiting
is almost over. It's ten seconds to nine o'clock.
The marchers chant: "10—9—8—7—6—5—4—3—2—1—"

A roar goes up from everyone. "Let's have
a parade!"

For three hours, New York City is full of magic.

There is a special link between marchers and watchers. Without the crowd, the parade would be empty.

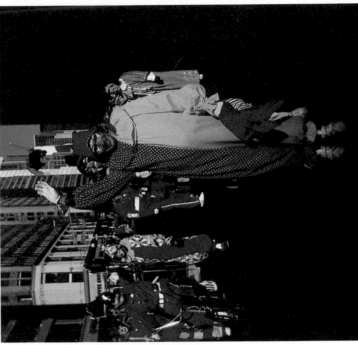

Every block, a performance for a new audience. The bands provide the rhythm; music is the spirit of happiness. All the effort, all the hard training and difficulties fade from the marchers' minds—today is a time for enjoyment. A parade is truly a time for enjoyment. A parade is truly a celebration.

The balloons can be seen as far as a mile away, in between the canyons of steel. Balloon handlers try to "read" the wind, as they tug their giants through the sky.

It's "Raggedy Ann's" first parade.

As each unit of the parade arrives at Herald Square, there is a performance for the NBC cameras. The Marching Millionaires have two minutes to play their hearts out for a television audience of tens of millions. They do it like . . . champions.

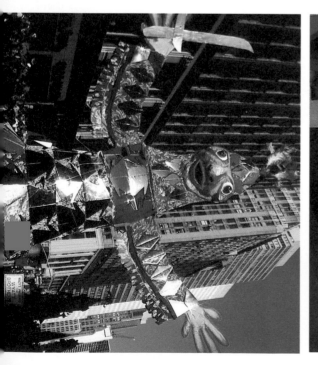

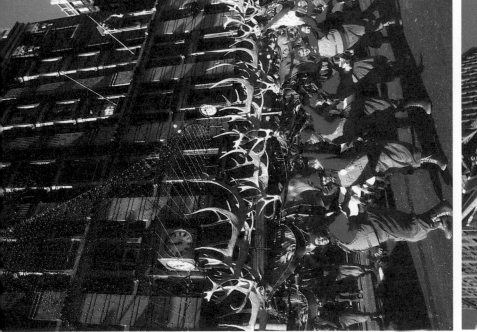

Just when you think you've seen all the tricks in the parade's magic box, another float or band or balloon comes along, brighter and more beautiful than the last.

But, wait. Can the parade be near the end already? Here comes…

Santa Claus! Riding on a swan carriage, with his elfin helpers around him, he moves grandly down the street. And then, in a moment, the parade is over...for *this* year.